FAB (Friends Against Bullying) Club is a book about how the best club, *ever*, got started.

Another book you might like is *Arctic Circle Comics: An Introduction.*

Some younger people you know might like *Hoover the Hungry Dog.*

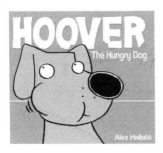

You can read more about these books, comics and other cool stuff by Alex Hallatt, at her website, alexhallatt.com.

INTRODUCING:

Ruth Wilkinson:
Ruth is happy to do stuff on her own or hang out with her dog, Arrow. When she isn't out climbing trees or riding her bike, she likes drawing.

Nancy Wong:
Nancy doesn't mind being known as a teacher's pet and loves studying, especially computers.

Toby Wilson:
Toby is picked on for his size and meekness. He would rather be at home making amazing buildings with his Lego.

Jake Blake:
Jake has his own style and doesn't care about fashion or what other people think.

Ravi Gupta:
Ravi loves reading and works hard at school. Unlike Nancy, he tries not to draw attention to himself. He wishes everyone would play by the rules.

Dave Howard:
Dave thinks he looks cool, but his clothes and hair look like they need a wash.

Trevor Skudder:
Trevor is big and strong, but doesn't like to fight. He joined Dave's gang because Ivan made him.

Ivan Carter:
Ivan looks up to Dave like a brother. He'd rather be at Dave's place or anywhere else than be at home.

FAB
(FRIENDS AGAINST BULLYING) CLUB

BY ALEX HALLATT

MOONTOON PUBLISHING

FAB Club
(members only)

To all my friends and everyone who has helped in the making of this book. Particularly, Jane, Steph, Izzie, William, Jo, Duncan, Dale, Debbie, Cathy, Lemon, Ali, Laila, John, Jules, Shubha, Vicki, Jackson, LJ, Zoey, Bodil and Ciadh.

Thanks also to Donna and her class at Thrupp Primary School: Freddie, another Freddie, Tom, Thomas, Corin, Megan, Lois, Tia, Sam, Amelia, Karl, Lauren, Archie, Georgia, Hannah, Mia, Max, Jonah, Lewis, Tilly, Ellis, Rowan, Zak, Blaine & Aaron. Freddie, Freddie, Tom, Thomas, Corin, Megan, Lois, Tia, Sam, Amelia, Karl, Lauren, Archie, Georgia, Hannah, Mia, Max, Jonah, Lewis, Tilly, Ellis, Rowan, Zak, Blaine and Aaron. They reviewed an early draft of the book and contributed to much of the food in Chapter 6.

CHAPTERS

CHAPTER ONE

A BIKE, A BUS AND SOME BULLIES

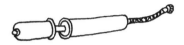

Ruth was better on a bicycle than any kid she knew. She could do wheelies and a skid stop, and could jump over 3 cousins (until her mum told her that was definitely not allowed). She could ride faster than the boys, even without her hands on the handlebars.

Ruth loved her bike. Unfortunately for Ruth, her mum thought riding to school was too dangerous. But she didn't know what the school bus driver was like. When you got

on the bus, you had to sit down quickly before Mrs Kawners, the driver, hit the accelerator, otherwise you ended up being launched into the back seat by the G force. She was even worse at slowing down and just as you thought she was going to run a red light, she would brake so hard that anything you didn't hold on to would catapult into the front windscreen.

Mrs Kawners drove as if she was running late for something really important. It wasn't. It was only school and they were never late... worst luck.

The good thing about the bus was that Ruth got to sit next to Amanda. She was two years older than Ruth and she had a Saturday job at a magazine store. She always had a stack of magazines that were perfect, except for their missing covers. Amanda loved the ones about pop stars, especially Andy Armarda. Her crush on him was funny, because she said he was the man she was going to marry. Ruth thought

sounded ridiculous. Amanda thought it sounded cool but what did Ruth know - she was just a kid.

Amanda insisted on sitting near the back, because she said,

said Ruth, looking at the boys on the back seat.

Ruth didn't want to know him. Dave had lank, dark hair, which hung across his face like a mouldy, wet shower curtain. He was a big fan of skulls and chains and black t-shirts.

Dave hung out with Trevor and Ivan. Trevor was the biggest kid in the school. He towered over all the other kids. Ivan was quite the opposite, but what he lacked in size, he made up for in sheer meanness. He tortured any creature he could get his bony hands on. Especially flies. Even if you don't like flies, it's cruel to rip their wings off.

One lunchtime, Trevor stopped Ivan from smashing some little kid's glasses and Ivan was furious. He punched Trevor in the stomach so hard that you could hear the whole playground gasp.

The only one who got to tell Ivan what to do was Dave. Ivan worshipped him like a god, which suited Dave just fine. Dave thought he was King of the Bus and sat in the middle of the back seat like it was his throne. Trevor and Ivan sat either side of him, like a pair of court jesters. Ruth imagined them wearing the silly outfits and it made her giggle.

When Ruth got to school, she bolted for the trees at the bottom of the playing field. She was tall enough to reach the lower branches and pull herself up. Then she climbed up where no one bothered to look and waited in her own world for the bell to ring. Often, kids would gather below the trees. She got to hear the secrets of the school. One day, Dave's gang even passed around a cigarette they had found. That day she heard a lot of coughing. Why cigarettes were cool was beyond her.

14

When the school bell rang, she loped up the field to the main doors and jumped in just before they closed. She liked to be unnoticed, remain *under-the-radar*, as her dad said.

Ruth didn't hate school, but she didn't like it either.

School was a series of endurance tests:

Test 1: Sitting through the boring classes, like History.

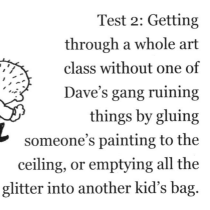

Test 2: Getting through a whole art class without one of Dave's gang ruining things by gluing someone's painting to the ceiling, or emptying all the glitter into another kid's bag.

Test 3. Eating your lunch in peace without having to trade the good stuff for a horrible meat paste sandwich that a knucklehead had stolen off someone.

Test 4: Trying not to answer too many questions, even if you know you are the only one who knows the answer, because no one likes a teacher's pet. This was completely obvious when Nancy put up her hand to every other question.

Nancy doesn't care if people think she's a teacher's pet, but she does care when she opens her locker and finds Dave's gang have squirted a whole bottle of ketchup into it.

Test 5: Making sure you don't stand out in other ways. Like Jake. Jake never said anything in class, unless he had to, but he didn't blend into the background like Ruth.

Dave didn't know what to do with Jake, because nothing really bothered him. He didn't even care when they called him "weirdo," or "gayboy" or "stinkyfartbutt."

Jake's smile just got bigger and bigger and that made Dave's gang mad. Especially Ivan. Ivan would find a way to wipe that smile off his face for sure.

CHAPTER TWO

AN INVITATION, MIXED TAPES AND
A SECRET

Ruth got on the bus the next day as usual. Amanda was bleating on about Andy Armarda as always. Mrs Kawners swerved to miss a squirrel and collected a corner shop's A-board. It remained attached to the front of the bus until Alan Butsnark pleaded with Mrs Kawners to stop to remove it, as he couldn't stand the scraping noise any more.

"I wonder who put that there," said Mrs Kawners, with surprise.

Meanwhile, Dave's gang were using peashooters to fire gobby paper balls at everyone. Amanda insisted they were far enough away to be safe, but Ruth felt a slimy sting on the back of her neck.

"Ow!"

she said. "That hurt!" She looked around at Dave's gang, who were laughing.

Except for Dave. He stood up and walked down the aisle towards the girls.

"Sorry, Ruth," he said. "I didn't mean to hit you... You know, I like, like you..."

"Well, you've got a funny way of showing it," said Ruth.

"Yeah. Heh. Heh." He laughed and then stopped when he saw that Ruth was still mad.

"Look, why don't I show it by taking you to the movies on Friday? Randomly Rearranging Robots 4 is on."

Now it was Ruth's turn to laugh.

"You've got to be joking," she said.

The truth was, she didn't want to go to any movie with Dave, but she watched his face turn from his version of charming to plain sad. She had upset him and she felt bad.

She tried to soften the blow by adding "I've heard that film's rubbish."

But it was too late, as Dave wasn't listening to her anymore. He was walking to the back of the bus with a face like thunder. Ruth was glad they were at the school gates and rushed off the bus before Amanda could tease her.

Ruth's first class was history. She didn't mind it, as Mr Senchurry told some good stories, and he allowed her to boost her grades by drawing illustrations in her homework. As she sat down, she saw that Ravi was surrounded by piles of paper.

"What are you doing, Rav?"

"It's my textbook. I was unpacking my bag when it dropped out on Ivan's foot and he went nuts. Dave got Trevor to rip the binding off and Ivan threw the pages all over the place. I'm trying to put it back in order," Ravi replied.

"Oh. Right."

Ravi asked her, "Have you seen Jake?"

"No. Doesn't he sit next to you?"

"Yeah. Okay...don't worry."

But Ravi did worry. History was the one subject Jake always turned up to. When the bell rang, Ravi was the first out and the first to find Jake. He was in the locker room, slumped against the wall. Ivan had found a way to get to him. Jake had sealed his own locker with silicone putty, but that didn't stop Ivan. Ivan had unscrewed the door and taken it off its hinges. When Jake came back to it, he found his entire collection of 1980s mix tapes had been pulled out of their cassettes. They were strewn all over the hall like a giant spider web.

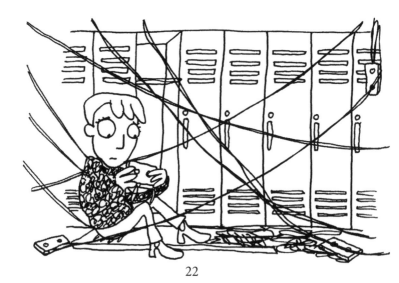

Ravi was really sad when he saw that, as he knew those tapes had belonged to Jake's dad, who wasn't around any more.

"We'll get our own back, Jake, don't worry," said Ravi, as he put the ruined tape into a pile.

"How? Those knuckleheads get away with everything. I'm sick of it!" Jake said and stormed out into the playground.

"We'll think of something, Jake. We're not like them. We've got brains!" As Ravi said this, he began to think of a way they could beat Dave's gang.

Jake walked over to the fence by the field and stared up at the sky.

He muttered a few words he wasn't allowed to say out loud and then began to calm down as he watched the birds flying overhead. It was then that he became aware of someone crying. It was Toby, who was sitting by the goal posts, bawling into his backpack.

Jake walked over and asked what was wrong.

"They took my lunch money. They always take my lunch money. I can't remember the last time I got to have lunch in school."

"Why don't you bring a packed lunch?" asked Jake.

"They'd take that too."

"Not if they didn't like it. You need to find something you like that they wouldn't."

"Like what?"

"I adore peanut butter, salad and sweet chilli sauce wraps."

"Eewwww... that sounds gross! No wonder they don't steal those!"

Jake reached into his satchel and pulled out a wrap. He gave half to Toby. "Have a bite."

Toby took a bite and prepared himself for the horrible taste but he really, really liked it. "That tastes delicious!"

"Sssshhhh! Don't tell them that, or they'll want some. Can you keep a secret?" asked Jake.

"Yes. Yes, I can."

"Good," said Ravi, who had crept up behind

them. "There's something else I want to tell both of you…"

CHAPTER THREE

THE FAB THREE: TOBY, RAVI AND JAKE

Ruth knew *something* was up when she noticed changes in three of the kids at school.

Toby had always tried to hide himself in the smallest corner of wherever he was. When Ruth did see him, he often looked red eyed and fearful, like a sick rabbit. And he never ate any lunch. But now Toby was looking less scrawny and less afraid. Though if you hid behind the bike shed and jumped out at him, he would still leap three feet in the air. Ruth saw Jake do that to him and after Toby had recovered, he actually laughed and punched Jake in the arm.

Not very hard, admittedly, but
Ruth was shocked to see him
touch anyone
at all.

Ravi had always been a grade A student.
Unlike Nancy, he was quiet in class and never
put his hand up, but he always had the answers
when he got asked by a teacher. He even knew
stuff that wasn't in their class textbooks. Now he
was still getting A grades, but he seemed to have
a life outside of his books. Ruth was surprised to
see him playing conkers in the playground. His
conkers were totally destroyed, but at least he
was playing.

Jake always seemed happiest in his own company, in his own world, with his headphones on. Now Ruth kept seeing him either with Toby, or Ravi, or both. Ravi and Toby had eaten peanut butter sandwiches for a week and used the lunch money they'd saved to buy an mp3 player.

Then they downloaded all of of the tracks that Jake had had on his mix tapes, put them on the player, and gave it to Jake. He was happy to have his music back, but Ruth didn't see him playing it at school anymore. Instead, Ruth saw him talking to Toby and Ravi more often than not.

The biggest change in all of them was that they looked happy. Really, really happy.

One day, the three boys were whispering by the water fountain. Ruth's curiosity got the better of her, and she approached them.

"What are you guys talking about?"

"Nothing," said Jake.

Ruth looked at Ravi, but he said, "Nothing."

Toby didn't speak at all.

"Oh come on... you are always whispering away, having secret little pow-wows. And it seems that every time any one of Dave's gang gets near one of you, the other two appear out of nowhere."

"You've noticed that," said Ravi, grinning.

Ravi had suggested to Jake and Toby that they put each other's phone numbers on speed dial. Then they could summon help at the touch of a button.

"Hang on," said Jake and he took the other two aside for another one of their little pow-wows. After a couple of minutes of discussion, they came back over.

"Okay, you're in," said Ravi.

"In what?" asked Ruth.

"We'd like to invite you to join our club," said Jake.

"What club?" asked Ruth.

"FAB - Friends Against Bullying."

"I'm not being bullied."

"But you don't <u>like</u> bullies, do you?"

"No, but I don't want to draw their attention to me either. You may be getting away with it now, but once Dave's gang work out what you're doing, they'll do everything they can to stop it."

"That's why it would be good to have more members," said Toby.

"Look, I'm glad this is working for you right now, but I don't need to hang out with a bunch of -" Ruth stopped herself saying 'losers', but her expression was all the boys needed to see.

"Suit yourself, Ruth," said Ravi as he turned to walk away.

Jake and Toby walked with him.

Ruth felt a bit rotten.

CHAPTER FOUR

SPIT PELLETS, STINK BOMBS AND A RUDE NOTE

At the end of the school day, Ruth ran out of the building, down the steps and across the playground. The bell had barely stopped ringing by the time Ruth got to the school gates. Her mum liked to pick her up after her shift at the sandwich factory had ended.

"58 seconds - a new record... did you cheat?" her mum asked.

"No!" said Ruth "Hey, I'm really hungry - what have you got?"

"Half a dozen packets of corned beef with fish paste."

"That's revolting!"

"Yes, there was a bit of a mix up on line three. Or it might have been deliberate. Deirdre and the manager seem to have had a lovers' quarrel. I think this was her way of getting her own back."

"Whatever, Mum... but I can't eat them. You'll have to give them to Arrow."

"What are **you** going to have for tea? Dog food?"

"It'd be better than those sandwiches!"

Arrow loved the sandwiches. Ruth was happy to eat boiled eggs and soldiers.

Ruth got on the bus the next day, ran up the stairs to the top and went to sit next to Amanda, but her backpack was on the seat beside her.

"Sorry, that seat's taken," said Amanda, looking straight ahead.

"What? Who's taken the seat?"

"Dave."

"Dave? Dave-the-knucklehead-at-the-back-of-the-bus, Dave?"

"He's not a knucklehead. He's sweet. He took me to the movies last night."

"To see *Randomly Reassembling Robots 4*? That's the worst film ever!"

"We didn't watch most of the film…"

"Gross!" grimaced Ruth.

At that moment, Dave shouted the order, "NOW!"

And a rain of soggy paper spit pellets pelted Ruth. She ran back down the stairs and looked out at a sea of little kids who stared at her school sweatshirt. It was covered in mushy bits of paper. Ruth squinted her eyes at the kids, daring them to say anything. They didn't. She turned her back on them and stood by the luggage rack, picking off pellets until she got to school.

She knew something was wrong with her locker before she got there. The whole corridor stunk and kids were running around holding their noses saying, "Eeuw! It stinks!" and other words to that effect. Ruth opened the locker door and was almost knocked back by the smell.

She saw the tell-tale signs of a dozen or more broken stink bomb capsules at the bottom of her locker. She held her nose, grabbed some books and ran to her class. Then she sat down and stashed her coat below her seat before anyone came in. It was Maths, which she was rubbish at.

"Well, hello, Ruth," said Miss Daykin, as she put her papers on her desk. "What a pleasure it is to see you here so early."

Ruth smiled at her as she opened her textbook and got a whiff of rotten eggs. Kids began to fill up the other seats as the teacher wrote some equations on the board. Almost immediately, giggling spread from table to table until it reached Ruth with a folded piece of paper. She opened it to find a less than flattering drawing of herself with a big stinking bottom.

The giggling got louder and Miss Daykin turned from the board.

"What's so funny, class?"

Ruth folded the paper, but was too slow to get it in her pocket.

"Bring it here please, Ruth."

She walked to the front of the class and handed it to the teacher. Miss Daykin glanced at it and snapped, "Stay behind after class. Now back to your seat."

After class, Ruth sloped back to the front of the class, as the rest of the kids laughed and bundled out. Miss Daykin waited until they were out of earshot and asked, "Are you okay, Ruth?" Ruth wasn't expecting sympathy and had to squeeze back tears with a frown.

"I'm fine, Miss."
"Because, if you're not, you can always come and talk to me, okay?"
"Yes, Miss."

"Okay. Well, run along."

Ruth went to her next class and thought about what she would do. She could talk to Miss Daykin, or another teacher. She could tell her mum. But what could any of them do? It was her own fault. She offended Dave and now she was paying for it. She just hoped things would calm down and he would forget about her and move on to someone else.

For the next couple of days, Ruth got onto the bus and stood by the luggage rack. But the driver told her she couldn't stand up if there were seats available. She didn't want to sit with the little kids, so she went upstairs and tried to talk to Dave.

"Look, Dave, I'm sorry..."

"What's that? Did someone hear a whining sound?"

Dave's gang laughed, and Dave gave Ruth a look that would have wilted flowers.

She would have to sit on the bottom deck. Ruth walked towards the back of the bus and saw that Ravi was squeezed into a corner.

"Oh... hi, Ravi - I didn't know you took this bus."

"Yup," said Ravi and continued to read his book.

"Mind if I sit next to you?"

"Nope," he said, still reading his book.

"I'm sorry."

He carried on reading.

"I was a bit of a...you know...when you asked if I'd like to join your club..."

"Yes..?"

"I was an idiot. And I really am sorry. And if the offer is still there, I'd like to join FAB."

CHAPTER FIVE

FAB FOUR, FAB RULES AND FAB PLANS

Ravi didn't say anything for ages as he looked down at his book.

Then he said, "Okay...maybe."

"Maybe?"

"Maybe. I'll have to ask the others," he said, as the bus stopped and they went into school. "I'll talk to you at lunch."

The morning dragged. When Ruth went out in the playground at lunchtime, she saw that Ravi was with Toby and Jake. They waved at her to come over.

"Hi, guys! Am I in?"

"You're in," said Jake, as Toby nodded.

Ravi added, "But there are certain conditions."

"Okay, what?"

The boys went through FAB's rules:

FAB Club Rules

Fab

1. Don't be a bully.
2. Help people who are being bullied.
3. Have fun.
4. Only FAB members are allowed in the clubhouse.
5. Password must be used to enter clubhouse.
6. No-one is to talk about FAB club outside FAB club.

Ravi Jake TOBY

"Alright," said Ruth, "those sound cool."

"If you agree to those rules, you'll have to sign this," said Ravi. He gave Ruth the piece of paper which had the rules and the logo of a big thumbs up.

"I'll sign it, but I don't like the logo. It's rubbish!"

"It's not really a logo," said Jake. "We can get rid of it, if you like."

"No, we've got to have a logo. Even Dave's gang has a logo," said Ravi.

"They do?" asked Jake.

"Yeah," said Ruth. "It's a V. They've all got a little V tattooed on their arms."

"Ouch! Let's not get tattoos," said Toby, looking worried.

"Why a V?" asked Jake. "DaVe, TreVor and IVan," explained Ravi.

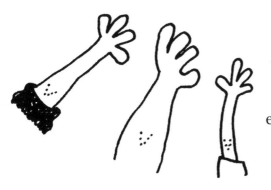

"Oh... that's kind of clever... for a knucklehead," said Jake.

Ruth pointed out, "Yes, but it means that no one else can join their gang unless they have a V in their name. So Ravi could join."

"Never in a million years!" protested Ravi.

"Okay, but they could recruit people called Vera,"

"or...Verruca,"

"or Vomit!!!"

They all laughed.

"Right, we won't get tattoos, but maybe you can work on a logo for us?" said Jake, smiling at Ruth.

"Sure," said Ruth "I'll have a think about that," and she signed the paper to become the fourth member of FAB.

"Now that I'm a member, can I see the clubhouse?" she asked.

"Um… we don't have a clubhouse," mumbled Ravi.

"What? It's in your rules, numbers 4 and 5!"

"I know," said Jake. "We want to have a clubhouse, but we don't know where to start."

The bell rang and the FAB club joined the other kids in their afternoon lessons. During the lessons, Ruth daydreamed of clubhouses.

When she met her mum at the gate, she was bubbling with excitement.

"Hi, Mum!"

"Well, you've cheered up."

"Yes! I've joined a club..." Then Ruth remembered Rule Number 6. "Er... it's a homework club."

"Really?"

"Yes. But there's a problem."

"What?"

"We don't have anywhere to do our homework together."

Ruth told her mum what she needed. She was so happy to see her smiling again that she agreed straight away. There was plenty of room at the bottom of the garden and a large oak tree. The tree would be strong enough to support a decent-sized tree house. Ruth's mum called Uncle Tony, who said he'd be happy to help. He could bring all the tools and fixings they would need.

All Uncle Tony asked was that Ruth and her friends should supply the wood.

"No problem," said Ruth to her mum.

She went to bed dreaming of being in the trees.

When Ruth got on the bus the next day, she could barely contain her excitement. She ran to sit next to Ravi, but a snotty little kid was already there.

"Beat it, kid," she said.

"Hey!" said the kid.

Ruth was about to drag him off the seat when Ravi hissed at her, "Rule Number 1."

"Oops! Sorry, kid. Look, Ravi, I need to talk to you: all of you. Can you arrange a meeting?"

"Sure," said Ravi and he sent messages to the other FAB members. They messaged back. "Okay. Break time by the goalposts."

"Excellent! See you then," said Ruth, smiling at Ravi.

CHAPTER SIX

THE FAB TREE HOUSE

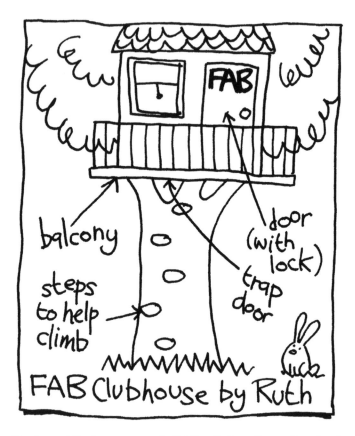

balcony

door (with lock)

steps to help climb

trap door

FAB Clubhouse by Ruth

Ruth told the rest of FAB club what she had arranged and they were all as excited as her. Except for Toby.

"I'm rubbish at climbing trees," he said.

"Don't worry," said Ruth, "we can put in a rope ladder." She showed them her plan.

"What about when we're building it? Before there's any rope ladder." said Toby.

"You can be ground crew," said Jake.

"Yeah, you can pass up the tools," said Ruth.

"And the refreshments," added Ravi.

"But before we get started, we need to find some wood," Ruth reminded them.

Each day after school, FAB combed the neighbourhood for wood. They found it in all sorts of places...in skips...

...and by
rubbish
bins...

...down by the river...

But a lot of it was rotten, or was full of rusty nails, or was oddly shaped. They needed to get some good stuff.

Then Toby had the bright idea of putting up a notice around the neighbourhood.

Shortly after that, they were given more old planks, doors and windows than they knew what to do with. They had to take all the notices down.

They were now ready to build the tree house.

Uncle Tony arrived at the weekend and they worked all day on Saturday.

Sorting and cutting the wood to size...

...putting in the floor and the bracing...

...eating an assortment of sandwiches, with crisps, chocolate biscuits and fruit for lunch...

...adding the walls with the doors, decking and windows...

They stopped when Ruth's mum called them in for dinner. She had made lots of different pizzas: ham and cheese, mushroom, pepperoni and onion, and tuna and sweet corn (Ruth's favourite).

The tree house crew was so hungry that it polished them off in no time. They had apple crumble and ice cream for dessert before they went off to bed. Ruth cleaned her teeth and then climbed the stairs to her bedroom. She could hear the boys talking as they settled into their sleeping bags in the lounge, and she thought it might be more fun to sleep down there too. But they soon became quiet as the tiredness of the day overtook them. Ruth fell asleep not a minute later. It seemed that immediately after that, her mum woke her up.

"You better get up quickly if you want any pancakes. The boys are wolfing them down," her mum said.

Ruth was up like a shot. She put on her clothes and flew down the stairs.

"Good morning, slugabed!" said Uncle Tony, as he ate the last of a fourth pancake.

"Did you leave any for me?" asked Ruth, seeing that the rest of FAB had left the table and headed outside.

"Don't worry; there are three keeping warm in the oven," said her mum.

Ruth made fast work of catching up and headed into the garden after washing down the last pancake with a big glass of orange juice.

"It's lucky it didn't rain last night," said Uncle Tony as they started to put on the roof.

It took them the entire morning to finish it, breaking only for a short morning tea break of milk shakes and chocolate chip biscuits.

Ravi, Jake and Toby's parents came over for lunch and Tony and FAB stopped working to join them for a big picnic on the lawn.

There were mini-pies, quiche, sausage rolls, salad, tuna sandwiches, egg and cress sandwiches, ham sandwiches, pasta salad, hotdogs, water melon, pineapple, raspberries, blueberries, apples, cheese, carrot sticks, tortilla chips and dips. Jake's mum had made elderflower cordial, which sounded weird, but tasted really nice. She had also made ginger beer, which tasted great, but had enough proper ginger to "knock your socks off," as Tony said. They finished with a dessert of jam doughnuts, vanilla slices and strawberries with chocolate sauce.

They were impossible to eat without getting very messy. Ruth's mum had to bring out a bucket of warm water for them to clean up before they got back to work.

With each of them armed with a brush, it didn't take long to paint the doors and windows and put weather-proof varnish on the rest of the wood. It took longer for them to clean the paint and varnish off themselves and get it out of their hair.

After they cleaned up, they came back out for a barbecue and toasted the tree house with fruit juice cocktails. The FAB clubhouse was ready and it was perfect.

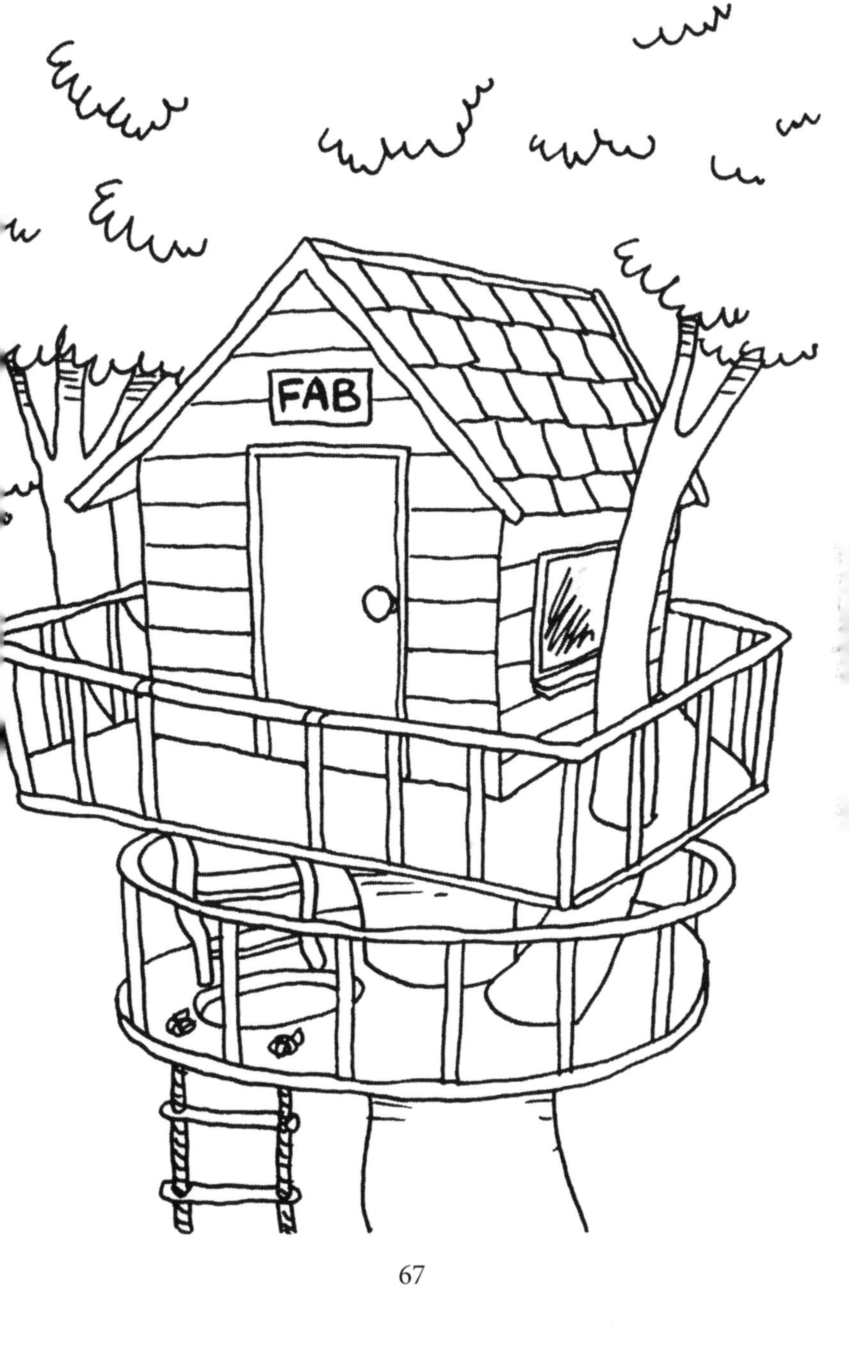
FAB

CHAPTER SEVEN

NANCY, FAB AND A FIRE

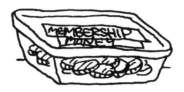

Nearly every day after school and most weekends, the FAB club met in the tree house. They did do **some** homework so that their parents didn't ask questions. But mostly they played games, read comics or just hung out.

Ruth did a lot of drawing. She was trying to come up with a logo, but none of them looked right.

"What is the FAB club about?" she asked the others.

"We're against bullying," said Ravi.

"Yes, but how? We aren't doing anything apart from being friends."

"We aren't being bullied anymore," said Toby.

It was true. Ruth now always sat with Ravi on the bus. When they were in school they rarely got pestered by Dave's gang, as they were able to call for help if they did.

Dave's gang didn't bully the members of FAB any more, but they didn't stop bullying others.

They tripped little kids up,

pulled one girl's hair so hard some of it came out,

and made fun of a new kid's clothes, which really wasn't fair, as his mum and dad didn't have much money.

YOU LOOK DORKY!

Once a month, Ravi collected membership money from each FAB club member. They used some of the money to buy the school handyman a big tin of biscuits. In return, he reinforced their lockers to make them almost impossible to break into.

Dave's gang moved on to other kids' lockers.

"Dave's gang are still being horrible to other kids," said Ruth, "and if we are Friends Against Bullying, shouldn't we be doing something about that?"

"We've tried talking to the other kids, but they are too scared to join us," said Jake.

"Or their parents won't let them out after school," said Ravi. This was true for Nancy.

Nancy ignored Dave's gang when they called her names. But ignoring them didn't make them stop.

Ruth had seen Dave's gang cornering Nancy in the playground and called the rest of FAB to come and help. They walked over and Trevor turned and saw them.

"Come on, Dave. Let's go," he said and the other two boys moved away from Nancy.

"Yeah," said Dave, "we don't want to hang out with *losers*, do we?" They walked away laughing.

"What was that all about?" Jake asked Nancy.

"Nothing. They wanted to look inside my backpack, that's all," said Nancy.

"That won't be all. They'll be up to something," said Ravi. "Why don't you join FAB, Nancy?"

"I've told you before; my dad likes me at home, studying. Anyway, I'm fine. I can look after myself."

The bell rang for afternoon classes. Nancy zipped up her backpack and hefted it onto her shoulders to walk back into the school building.

"Whatever she has in that backpack, it sure is heavy," said Ruth.

"And Dave's gang want it," said Jake.

Ruth went to bed that night, trying to think of how FAB could stop kids being bullied, even if they didn't want to join FAB. She dreamt they were superheroes, swooping in to foil the bullies. Police sirens blared as Dave's gang were taken away for crimes against kids.

The sirens were so loud that they woke Ruth up. She wasn't dreaming anymore. Ruth jumped out of bed and looked out of the window. The tree house was on fire.

She ran to her mum's room and woke her up. They both went downstairs, put on their coats and stepped out of the back door. Even though the tree house was at the bottom of the garden, they could feel the heat of the flames. A fire engine had arrived at the bottom lane and firemen were running to get a hose to the tree.

Their neighbour, Gary, walked over to them.

"Are you two alright?" he asked.

"Yes," said Ruth's mum.

"No," said Ruth, "that was our clubhouse."

"Sorry, kid," said Gary. "I saw it when I was driving back from my nightshift. I called the fire brigade, but it was already well alight."

They watched the firemen bring the blaze under control. After about half an hour, the fire was out, but Ruth could see that the damage was done. All that was left of the clubhouse were charred bits of wood and ashes.

CHAPTER EIGHT

FAB CLUB RISES FROM THE ASHES

Ruth's mum made everyone a cup of tea. She brought the tea out on a tray to the firemen, who were packing up their hoses.

"Thanks, love," said one of the firemen. He took a cup and added a crazy amount of sugar to it. "Have you any idea who might want to burn down your tree house?"

"No," said Ruth's mum, with surprise, "why?"

"It looks like arson. We had a bit of a look around and found this in your side of the hedge, by the lane."

The fireman showed them a large petrol canister.

Ruth's mum had no idea who would do such a thing, but Ruth did. She didn't want to talk to her mum about it, because she would have to tell her all about FAB too. And she wasn't ready to do that. Not yet. Not until she had talked to the others.

"I'm tired, Mum. Can I go to bed?" Ruth asked, putting down the tea.

"Of course, darling. I'll be in in a little bit. You go on up."

Ruth went back to bed, but didn't sleep much. She had a lot to think about.

The next day, FAB met at the bottom of the playing field. Somehow, the news about the tree house burning down was already going around the school. There were even pictures of the fire on the Internet. They were taken before the fire engine arrived. Ruth told the others what had happened and what the fireman had told her.

"Those dirty rotten…"

said Jake.

"What are we going to do?" asked Toby.

"What can we do? It's over," said Ravi.

"What do you mean, 'it's over'?"' asked Ruth.

"The FAB club; they've destroyed it. Dave's gang saw what we were doing and they destroyed it."

"Nonsense," said Ruth. "They destroyed our clubhouse, but they haven't destroyed FAB."

"Yeah," said Jake, "we're still here."

"Yes!" said Toby, relieved.

"Where are we going to meet?" asked Ravi. "We can't just have our meetings in the school playground."

"Our parents still think we have a homework club, don't they?" said Ruth.

"Mum's cottoned on to the fact that we do more than just homework," said Ravi.

"Mine hasn't. Probably because my grades are now better!" said Jake.

"Mine too!" said Toby.

"Okay, so they won't mind if we take turns meeting in each other's bedrooms," said Ruth.

"Does that mean I have to tidy it?" said Toby.

"Yes!" said the other three, who knew how untidy Toby was.

FAB had their first meeting after the fire at Ruth's house. They could see the black stump of the tree from her bedroom window.

"Should we tell the police about Dave's gang? We know that they did it," said Ravi.

"Dave's smarter than you think," said Jake.

"He won't have left any fingerprints on that petrol can. Who knows if there's enough evidence to point the finger at them?"

"Sometimes it's better to lay low," said Toby. "We don't want to get them annoyed."

"What about us? Aren't we annoyed?" said Ruth, clearly annoyed.

Jake said, "Dave's gang didn't burn our clubhouse to annoy us. We've threatened their reign of knuckleheadom..."

"Is that a word?" interrupted Ravi.

"Dave's gang set out to destroy us, didn't they?" said Jake. "But we rose from the ashes."

"Yeah, like a phoenix," said Ravi.

"What's a phoenix?" asked Toby.

Ravi told them about the mythical creature. The ancient Greeks believed that this bird was not killed by fire, but rose from the ashes to be reborn, stronger than before. Ruth's eyes lit up and she started to draw. By the end of their meeting, she had designed a logo for the FAB club.

Everyone loved it, and she helped them all draw the logo onto their bags, notebooks and pencil cases. The FAB club had risen like a phoenix from the ashes and they were proud to show it. Kids at school asked them what the logo was for and they told them. They noticed that the logo began to appear on other kids' bags, even though they didn't attend the FAB club meetings. One day, Ruth was in the girls' loo and saw the logo had joined the graffiti on the wall. She was pretty sure none of the boys had put it there.

FAB was increasing in popularity, even if it was only an idea to most people who drew the logo on their stuff.

It was a powerful idea and it really annoyed Dave's gang. They scratched out as many logos as they could with their V sign. However, Ruth was glad to see the phoenix in the loo was untouched. Dave's gang could only reach so far.

CHAPTER NINE

THE FAB FIVE AND A STOLEN LAPTOP

It was a Sunday afternoon and the members of the FAB club were meeting in Toby's room. There was a knock on the door.

"Who's there?" asked Toby.

"Ahem!" coughed the door knocker.

"You're supposed to ask for the password," said Ravi.

"But we're all here," said Ruth.

"What's the point of a password, if we're never going to use it?" said Ravi.

"Okay, okay," said Jake. He then called out, "What's the password?"

"Underpants," said the door knocker.

"Underpants?" said Jake.

"That's right! Has no one else learned the password?" said Ravi, crossly. He was the one who made up a new password every week and sent it to FAB club members' phones.

"Underpants, underpants, under-pants!" shouted the door knocker.

Ravi opened the door to find Nancy.

"Oh, it's you," he said, "come in."

"How did you know our password?" asked Toby.

"And where we were?" added Ruth.

"Your security systems are rubbish," said Nancy. "I intercepted the messages on your phones to read your password. Then I used your phones' GPS signals to find you."

"Is it that easy?" asked Ruth, getting worried.

"No, it's not. Actually, I'm quite good at this," confessed Nancy.

"Okay, well done, Nancy. Now leave us alone. This is a private club meeting," said Ravi, who was extra cross that someone had finally used his password system, but shown it to be useless at the same time.

He was about to shove Nancy out of the door when she said, "Wait! I want to join the FAB club. I'm being bullied and I want to be a member of FAB."

"Let her in," said Ruth.

The FAB members went through the rules with Nancy, who agreed to them without much thought. She had other things to think about and needed FAB's help.

"Dave's gang have stolen my laptop," she said.

"Your security system is rubbish," said Ravi and immediately wished he hadn't. Nancy ignored him and continued.

"I was working in the school library and went to the toilet, just for a second. When I came out, it was gone."

"Well, anyone could have taken it," said Ruth.

"No way. I had it locked to the desk with a steel cable. They took it using bolt-cutters."

"Those things are like scissors on steroids," said Jake.

"Whoah! That's how they've been stealing the bikes from the school bike shed," said Ravi.

"Dave's dad is a locksmith. I bet Dave borrowed the bolt-cutters from him," said Jake.

"Maybe," said Ruth, "but how are we going to find your laptop now?"

"I've got a GPS tracker on it, of course. I used my phone to track where it went."

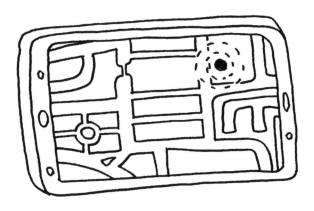

"Where is it?" asked Ruth.

"At Dave's place. In his dad's shed."

"Great!" said Ruth.

"What?" said Nancy.

"Great. This is proper evidence. It means we

can call the police and send them to Dave's place and—"

"No," said Nancy, "we can't call the police. The police can't know."

"Can't know what, Nancy?" asked Ravi.

"Look, I've been in trouble before for using a computer to hack into places."

"What places?" asked Jake.

"The library - I extended the return dates on all the books I borrowed by a few decades. The cinema - I could book tickets for any film for free! Though I still had to buy the blimmin' popcorn. I got busted when I tried to sort something out for our holidays. Every summer, we go to the same caravan site in Eastborington. I'm flippin' fed up of it - old folk in deck chairs, a rusty pier with rubbish amusements and a pebble beach with a sea that looks as inviting as a bath of cold sick.

I was making progress hacking into some travel sites to arrange for my parents to 'win' some tickets to fly to the Gold Coast, when it all went wrong.

The police barged in and were going to arrest my parents. When they found out that Mum and Dad couldn't even operate a microwave, they knew I was to blame. Luckily, they couldn't do anything to me directly, because I was so young. Unluckily, they could take away my computer. My parents banned me from using a computer again."

"How did you get the laptop?" asked Ruth.

"On the Internet, no one knows you're a kid," said Nancy. "I've been doing freelance coding work for years and stored up a lot of Bitcoins."

"Bits of coins?" said Toby, confused.

"Bitcoins. It's a type of Internet money," said Ruth.

"I used them to buy my laptop, the one that's gone missing," said Nancy.

"I understand why you don't want to go to the police," said Ruth.

"Don't worry," said Ravi, "you're in the FAB club now. We'll sort this out."

CHAPTER TEN

BIKES, INSULTS AND CRACKING A LOCK

The FAB club broke out the chocolate biscuits and blackcurrant cordial and worked out a plan.

"We have to get into that shed," said Jake.

"I've been there. It's locked," said Nancy.

"Oh," said Ruth, "that could be tricky."

"Not really," said Nancy. "I can get into combination locks if I have enough time. The problem is that Dave's gang are always hanging around. If I get caught, there's really going to be trouble."

"We could bunk off school," suggested Jake.

"No way!" said Ravi. "We'll end up in trouble with everyone if we do that."

Toby and Nancy nodded their heads in agreement.

"We need to distract them for long enough for

Nancy to break the combination," said Ravi.

"That's easy!" said Ruth. "I can do that. I'll buzz them on my bicycle; they'll never catch me if I'm on my bike."

"Yeah, that'll work," said Ravi. "But you'll have to make sure you don't go *too* fast. Otherwise they will give up the chase completely. You'll have to take a bit of a chance with them."

"No worries," said Ruth, "this will be fun!"

The FAB members discussed the finer points of the plan until all the biscuits and cordial had gone. They were ready.

Ruth went home to get her bike. Ravi and Jake enjoyed making a big banner out of an old sheet.

Nancy and Toby made sure their phones had the cameras set to video. They wanted to record everything that happened, whatever happened. Then they walked over to Dave's house. Nancy said she often saw Dave's gang sitting on the old sofa on the front lawn, but there was no one there. They stopped at the fence and listened.

Toby said, "They're playing computer games, I can hear them."

"I can't hear anything, Toby. Your ears are amazing!" said Jake and Toby smiled. Usually, people made fun of his ears, but now he was proud of them.

"There's Ruth," said Ravi, as he saw Ruth on her bike at the end of the street. "She's waiting for the signal. But how are we going to get Dave's gang outside?"

"Don't worry about that yet. Help me with the banner," said Jake and they unfurled the banner across the fence.

"Okay, now you all hide behind that van and I'll get them out," Jake said.

The other three dashed over and crouched behind the van as Jake walked over to the door, rang the bell and ran.

As he made for the van, he let out a loud whistle and signalled to Ruth, who began to bike down the road. Jake got behind the van, just as the front door opened.

Dave, Trevor and Ivan came bolting out of the house and through the gate. The first thing they saw was the banner. The next thing they saw was Ruth, who had stopped halfway down the road.

"Come here and say that," said Ivan as he and the other two grabbed the bikes that were leaning against the inside of the fence.

Ruth biked down to their gate and as she passed it, she turned slightly and hit the brakes. She skidded to a stop. From the knucklehead's angle, she looked like she had fallen off the bike, but the FAB members could see that she was still in control, ready to jump back up.

Dave's gang got onto their bikes and pedalled out of the gate. They nearly reached Ruth, but she sprang up and onto her pedals. She accelerated down the road, with them in hot pursuit.

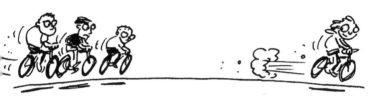

As they turned the corner of the road, the FAB members took their chance. They ran through the open gate and to the yard out back. Nancy grabbed the lock on the shed and started to turn the wheels of the combination. Ravi looked at his watch. Ruth planned to get the gang to the canal before she took off and lost them. She thought that was five minutes away, so Ravi was allowing ten minutes for the shed operation.

"One minute," he said, and then, "two minutes..."

"Shut up, Ravi," said Nancy, "I've got to concentrate."

Ravi kept quiet for another few minutes, but couldn't resist saying "six minutes..." when they passed the half way mark.

That was when Nancy said, "Got it!" and the lock sprang open.

They couldn't believe what they saw.

CHAPTER ELEVEN

INSIDE THE SHED

The shed was full of stuff: bikes, computers, TVs, phones and all sorts of things. Things that had gone missing from other kids' lockers. Things that didn't belong to Dave's dad or Dave's gang.

"Woah! That's my camera," said Jake, reaching into a box. "I thought I lost that a few months ago."

He grabbed it and showed it to Nancy and Toby, who started videoing everything with their phones. "Look, it's got my initials scratched on the bottom: 'JB'."

Jake put the camera in his pocket and took over the filming from Nancy. It didn't take long for her to find her laptop. She opened it up and it whirred into life.

Nancy tapped on the keyboard. "It looks like they didn't guess my password, thank goodness." She snapped the laptop shut and put it back in her backpack.

"Eleven minutes!" said Ravi. "We better go!"

The FAB club members left the remaining stuff in the shed and Nancy closed the door. She turned the combination lock numbers back to where they were before. They ran out the gate and up the road, turning left to the alleyway that led to the park. Ruth was waiting for them behind the kiosk.

"Phew! You took your time. I was getting worried."

"Don't worry, it all went to plan," said Jake.

"Except we were a minute late," said Ravi.

"It's lucky Dave's gang are so out of shape," said Ruth. "I really had to slow down on the way to the canal, otherwise I thought they'd never get there. But once I got to that bridge, I took off. Trevor and Dave gave up almost straight away after that, but Ivan kept coming for a while. I had to lose him with some pretty tricky cycling."

"Good job, Ruth," said Nancy, "and it was worth it. We got our stuff back."

"We?" asked Ruth.

Her friends explained what they found in the shed.

In the meantime, Nancy transferred the video from the two phones to the laptop.

"I'll edit this and send you the link when I'm done," she said.

"We'd better split," said Jake and the FAB club members went their separate ways.

Shortly after dinner, Ruth's phone buzzed in her pocket. She was watching a movie with her mum and waited until an advert break to go to the bathroom and check her phone.

The message simply gave a link to the video. Ruth clicked the link and saw that Nancy had done a great job of editing the video, with a suspenseful soundtrack and her voiceover explaining the footage. Ruth was shocked to see how much stuff had been stolen. She'd edited out all the shots of FAB club members, but Ruth knew that Dave's gang would know who was responsible if they saw it.

As if echoing her thoughts, a second message came through on her phone:

Nancy was a smart cookie. She wanted to make sure that it was seen at school after it was too late for Dave's gang to do anything about it. Unless they checked over the shed carefully, they should be none the wiser that FAB had been in there. And that was going to work to FAB's advantage.

CHAPTER TWELVE

THE FAB CROWD

Ruth was dying to get on the bus to talk to Ravi the next day, but before she could say anything, he put his finger to his lips and said, "Rule 6."

Ruth rolled her eyes. Ravi was such a stickler for the rules.

When they got off the bus, they saw Nancy, Jake and Toby by the monkey bars. They went

over and joined them, but none of them were talking either. They were all looking intently at their phones.

Then Nancy counted down, "10...9...8...7...6...5...4...3...2...1."

Their phones and phones all over the playground beeped.

"It worked!" said Jake.

Ruth looked at her phone and saw there was a message:

STOP THIEVES!

It was followed by the link to the video that Nancy had uploaded. Soon, everyone was clustered around people with phones, watching the video. Ruth could hear people shouting.

"That's my bike!" said one kid.

"That's my phone!" said another.

"That's my Snootykins!" said a little girl, crying her eyes out.

(Why Dave's gang had stolen an old, cuddly toy elephant was never explained.)

Ruth kept refreshing the video page on her phone. There were now hundreds and hundreds of views, as kids were sending the link to everyone they knew. She glanced up to see Trevor was hurrying towards them.

"Uh-oh," Ruth said.

The others looked up. They put their phones in their pockets and clustered together.

"I've seen your video," said Trevor.

"What video?" said Toby, which was a daft thing to ask, but it bought them more time.

"It's okay. I'm not out to get you. I'm glad that video is online."

"Really?" said Ruth, "but you stole all that stuff."

"I know. I didn't want to. Dave said his dad needed it and Ivan said I better help, or my life wouldn't be worth living."

"That sounds about right," said Ruth.

"So, what are you going to do about it now?" asked Jake.

"Two things. Firstly, I sent that link to the police and told them what happened."

"Wow, that's cool," said Ruth.

"Secondly, I'd... I'd like to join the FAB club."

"I'm happy for you to join," said Ruth, looking at the others. Jake, Nancy and Toby nodded. Ravi shot her a look and she continued, "Provided you agree to the rules, of course."

"We'll explain them to you later," said Jake, "but it looks like we've got company."

Dave and Ivan were walking over to them and they didn't look happy.

"We're going to beat you all up so that you are in the same sorry state we left your tree house in!" shouted Ivan.

"Sorry about that," said Trevor to Ruth.

"What are you doing over there, Trevor? Come here!" called Dave. Trevor stood his ground with the rest of FAB.

Meanwhile, the other kids in the playground were gathering around, just like they did any time there was a fight. This time they were all on the same side. They were all behind FAB.

Ivan ran towards FAB with his teeth bared
and his fists clenched. Dave wasn't far behind
him.

But before they could get to them, the crowd rushed forward shouting so much it was deafening. The video and years of bullying by Dave's gang had turned them into an angry mob.

Ivan and Dave knew they were outnumbered and turned and ran.

They ran towards the gates, where the police were walking in.

"Now, now, lads, what's the hurry?" one asked, as they grabbed them by the arms and marched them to the head teacher's office.

The FAB club members looked at each other and sighed with relief. None of them had really wanted to fight. As all the kids talked about what had happened, the bell rang and they drifted into the school building.

A little later, they were in Miss Terry's science class. Everyone was still babbling away about what happened in the playground, when Mr Meeners, the Deputy Head, entered the room.

"Quiet!" he boomed. Everyone fell silent. "Mrs Caning would like to see Trevor Skudder in her office, right away." There was a murmur. "The rest of you get back to work."

The rest of the FAB club didn't see Trevor in their other classes that day. When they met in the playground the next day, they found out that Dave and Ivan had been expelled.

"Phew!" said Toby, "but what happened to Trevor?"

"I hope he wasn't expelled too," said Nancy.

"No, I wasn't," said Trevor.

The rest of the FAB club turned to see Trevor, grinning from ear to ear. Ruth gave him a big hug and the other four joined in.

Then Trevor explained that, because he had changed his ways and stood up to the bullies, he wasn't expelled from school. But he did have to do community service like Dave and Ivan.

The police made sure that, piece by piece, the contents of the shed were returned to their rightful owners. They also investigated the eBay account of Dave's dad and discovered what had happened to some of the stolen things that weren't in the shed. He would be going to court later that month.

Trevor was going to give evidence at court. He would have been afraid, but he knew that the FAB club was behind him. His friends were also going to help him with his community service. That meant four weekends of cleaning off graffiti and picking up a lot of litter.

Ruth, Jake, Nancy, Ravi and Toby helped Trevor, so that he finished his jobs before lunch each Saturday.

And what did the FAB club do on the rest of those weekends?

They built their new clubhouse.

Hey - thank you for reading!

If you enjoyed *FAB Club*,
please leave me a review
saying what you liked
about the book. It will
help me write more books
about the FAB Club, like
*FAB Club 2 - Friends
Against Cyberbullying* .

My author page:
amazon.com/author/hallatt
Or look for me on GoodReads.

Cheers!

Alex

alexhallatt.com

FRIENDS AGAINST BULLYING
– JOIN THE CLUB!

Go to alexhallatt.com/fab and sign up for the real FAB Club (if you haven't already). Become a friend against bullying, get a certificate of membership and be the first to hear news of books, author events and more.

GLOSSARY

(WHAT WORDS MEAN)

I'm a British-Kiwi and this book is written with English English and New Zealand English readers in mind. Here are some words that you may not understand:

Biscuits - cookies

Boiled eggs and soldiers - the "soldiers" are the slices of buttered toast that you dip in the runny egg yolk - yum!

Brilliant - this means really good (it can also mean really smart)

Bunking off school - wagging school, or skiving school, or generally not going to school.

Conkers - horse chestnuts ("buckeyes" in American English)

Corner shop - a store on the corner. Often a convenience store selling things like newspapers, milk and bread.

Cottoned on - "to cotton on" means "to realise". I don't know why. English is a funny language.

Crisps - potato chips

Loo - toilet, dunny, WC, or bathroom

Maths - Americans shorten "mathematics" to "math". We don't.

Petrol - gasoline

Rubbish - really bad.

Rubbish bin - trash can

ALEX HALLATT

Alex Hallatt was born and brought up in the West Country in England. She emigrated to New Zealand, where she met her partner, Duncan and his dog, Billie. They spent a few years living in Australia, England & Spain and, at time of writing, are heading back to New Zealand, where Alex hopes to plant a garden, Duncan plans to do a lot more fishing and Billie plans to avoid having to go in the cargo hold of a plane ever again.

Alex was bullied at school, but found her friends and is now happy to be following the first three rules of FAB Club (though she is breaking Rule Number 6 a **lot**).

FAB Club Rules

1. Don't be a bully.
2. Help people who are being bullied.
3. Have fun.
4. Only FAB members are allowed in the clubhouse.
5. Password must be used to enter clubhouse.
6. No-one is to talk about FAB club outside FAB club.

One last thing.

If you, or someone you know, has been bullied in real life, you can get help. Talk to your family and talk to your teachers.

You can also go to the the FAB Club page, where there are links to helpful websites.
www.alexhallatt.com/fab

IF YOU ARE BEING BULLIED:

1. Tell someone. Talk to an adult you trust - a parent, a teacher, or a family friend.

2. It is not your fault. Don't blame yourself. There is never a good reason to bully other people.

3. Often bullies pick on kids who are different, but being different can be a good thing. If you are not being unkind to other people, you do not deserve other people being unkind to you.

4 You can make yourself less likely to be bullied. If you act confident, people will think you are confident and then you are likely to **become** confident!

Stand up tall, with your shoulders back (not in a crazy way - think of looking like a president and not like a chicken).

Take your time to reply to other kids. Look them in the eye and think of the right thing to say, which might just be "no". It may even be best to say nothing and walk away, or you might want to change the subject. Don't insult people, just show them that you are your own person and will not be bullied.

5. Don't make changes for other people - make them for yourself. Who do you want to be? What do you want to do in your life?

6. Find other interests that are fun for you. Ask an adult, if you want to find a club to join and other people who share your interests. In this way, you might find children who are more like you, who can become your friends.

Remember that friends make you feel good. They may not always agree with you, but they should support you. If you find that spending time with friends always makes you feel worse, it is time to make new friends.

CYBERBULLYING

If you are bullied online, or via your phone:

1. Tell someone. Report the bullying to the website administrator. If it continues, tell an adult you trust.

2. Do not reply to bullying remarks. Use website or app settings to block people who send you messages that upset you.

3. Make any online account private, so that you can only be contacted by friends and not strangers, or people you do not want to contact you.

4. If being online makes you unhappy, **stop**. Being online, or on your phone is not somewhere you have to be, like school. Ignore what other children say you should do, if it is not what you want to do. You are the boss of you.

IF YOU SEE SOMEONE ELSE BEING BULLIED:

1. If you feel safe in the situation, tell the bully that what they are doing isn't cool.

2. Invite the kid who is being bullied to hang out with you for a while.

3. If the problem continues, it is okay to tell a teacher, or an adult you trust.

REMEMBER THE FIRST THREE RULES OF FAB CLUB:

1. Don't be a bully.
2. Help people who are being bullied.
3. Have fun!

More information on FAB Club and bullying is at alexhallatt.com/fab.

And you can always write to me and be one of my friends who are against bullying.
Alex@alexhallatt.com

Printed in Great Britain
by Amazon